JILL & LION

Lesley Barnes

TATE PUBLISHING

Jill had just reached Dog's favourite part of the book.

'I can't read the ending of the story,' said Jill to Dog. 'The last words are all smudged!'

'I don't like the look of this,' thought Dog.

'Sorry,' sniffed a voice from the page.
'I just can't stop crying.'
The voice came from the Lion.

'What's wrong, Lion?'
asked Jill, who hated
to see anyone upset.

'The Ringmaster
stole me from the jungle,
took my King Hat and
brought me into this story.
I'm nothing without
my King Hat,'
said Lion to Jill.

'I used to rule the jungle,
now all I do is drive
around in tiny circles.'

Jill didn't like an unhappy ending
and without any hesitation, she swung
into the story with an almighty leap
and headed straight for the Ringmaster.

'I'll get your crown back, Lion!' she exclaimed.

'The crown!'
shouted the Ringmaster,
'she's got the crown!'

*But the acrobats were quicker
than Jill and they soon had her trapped!*

Dog was horrified!
His mistress was
in trouble!

*So bravely, he gathered up
all the strength he could muster
and bounded in after her.*

Dog distracted the acrobats
so that Jill could grab the crown.

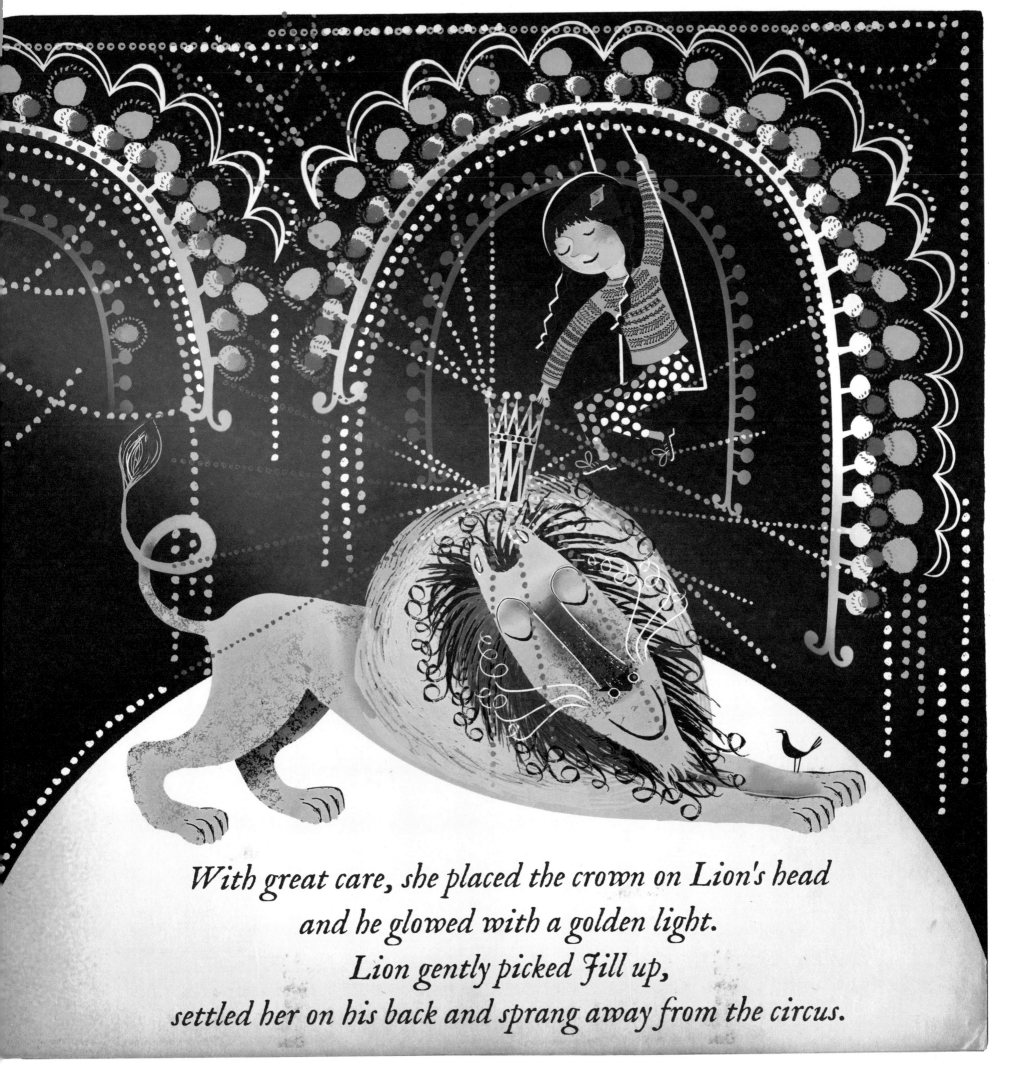

With great care, she placed the crown on Lion's head
and he glowed with a golden light.
Lion gently picked Jill up,
settled her on his back and sprang away from the circus.

'After them!'
screamed the Ringmaster
to the acrobats.

'Where are we going, Lion?'
Jill cried.

'To the circus train,' shouted Lion. 'We can make our escape to the jungle on it!'

Lion raced ahead to the train as Jill
and Dog held off the circus mob.

'Who's going to drive the train?'
shouted Jill to Dog.

'Neither of us has a driving licence!'

'Don't worry!'
roared Lion triumphantly.
'I'm a very experienced driver...
I've had lots of practice
in the clown car.'

THE
END

It was Lion!

'Onwards! Towards the jungle!'
shouted Jill, as the train thundered through the
last page of the circus story.

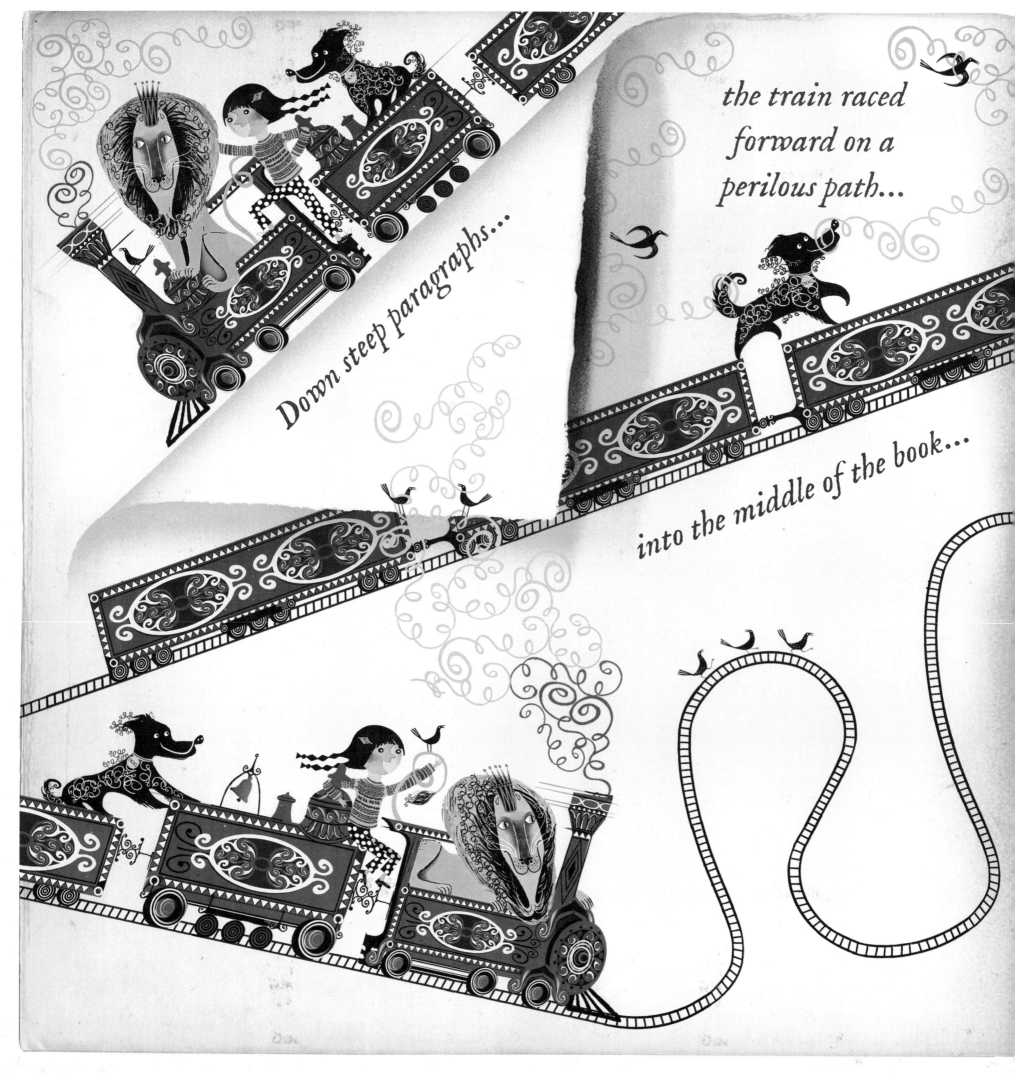

the train raced forward on a perilous path...

Down steep paragraphs...

into the middle of the book...

and out the other side...

around sharp sentences...

plummeting
through dark
tunnels...

faster and faster until...

Suddenly! A mighty gust of wind
blew the pages of Jill's book,
flinging the train around
like a rollercoaster!

'My King Hat!' roared Lion.

'I'm nothing without
my King Hat!'

For once, Jill didn't know what to do.
But Dog had spotted something
hiding in the page...

It was the driver's hat!

'You don't need a crown, Lion,' said Jill, placing the driver's hat on Lion's head. 'It's what's inside that makes you special and you make a fantastic train driver!'

Soon Jill, Dog and Lion had
the jungle in their sights.

THE JUNGLE KING

'I'm not the king of the jungle any more,' sighed Lion,
as he looked up at the title of his story.
Just then, Jill had a brilliant idea!
She stood on Lion's back and began to rearrange the letters.

THE JUNGLE TRAIN

The clever chimps added a few extra letters
so that the title read 'The Jungle Train'.
'You have a new beginning for your story now, Lion!' exclaimed Jill.
'And we can't wait to read the ending!'